JACK FROST

A CHRISTMAS NOVELLA

DEBBIE MACOMBER

Praise for Debbie Macomber's
bestselling Christmas novels

The Christmas Spirit

"Bestseller and Hallmark Channel stalwart Macomber (Dear Santa) does it again with a candy cane–sweet holiday romance about two friends who swap lives for a week before Christmas….An eclectic supporting cast—including cadres of strippers and bikers—and a comically disastrous climactic Christmas Eve church service make the narrative shine bright. It's exactly what readers want from a Macomber holiday outing." – *Publishers Weekly*

Dear Santa

"A sweet and simple holiday romance…a fun, fluffy holiday escape." – *Publisher Weekly, starred review*

Jingle All The Way

"This delightful Christmas story can be enjoyed any time of the year." – *New York Journal of Books*

"Jingle All The Way will hit the spot." – *Insider*

Alaskan Holiday

"Author Debbie Macomber is a pro, and "Alaskan Holiday" promises to melt any frozen heart." – *USA Today*

"This sweet seasonal story warmed up my chilly heart and had me smiling. Plus Josie and Palmer left me starry-eyed for days!" – *First for Women magazine*

Merry and Bright

"Online dating leads to hilarious, eventually romantic results for a deserving, likable pair in this tender holiday delight." – *Library Journal*

"Merry and Bright was a holiday romance with a completely engaging storyline and endearing characters, plus the added bonus of being filled with the warmth and spirit of the Season." –*Harlequin Junkie*

Twelve Days of Christmas

"...a delightful, charming read for anyone looking for an enjoyable Christmas novel.... Settle in with a warm blanket and a cup of hot chocolate, and curl up for some Christmas fun with Debbie Macomber's latest festive read." – *Bookreporter.com*

"Macomber's celebrated warmth and flair for storytelling make this a fun holiday frolic." – *Publishers Weekly*

.....

Copyright © 2023 by Debbie Macomber
All rights reserved.

Published in the United States
by Debbie Macomber Inc.

ISBN 979-8-9888953-1-2
Ebook 979-8-9888953-0-5

FIRST EDITION

Book Cover by Daniela Medina

DEDICATION

To
Gary and Shelly Snodgrass
For your advice and guidance.

LETTER TO READERS

Christmas 2023

Dear Friends,

For the past 26 years I've had a published Christmas book. Writing those stories has been some of the most fun I've had as an author. I've lost count of the number of times I've had to pause because I was laughing too hard to continue typing.

Because I'm practicing being retired, I thought I'd skip a Christmas book this year and discovered hard as I tried, I couldn't do it. You see I had this great idea and as great ideas are prone to do, it wouldn't leave me alone. And so, semi-retired or not, I turned to my keyboard and typed furiously to tell the tale of **Jack Frost**. And yes, I did laugh, which tells me you will as well.

My team has worked tirelessly to bring this story to you on a variety of platforms. Online, print, audio, and to them I am forever grateful. This is a whole new experience for us. The learning curve was helped along with my wonderful agent Theresa Park and her team.

Here it is, my friends, my 26th Christmas story and it is releasing on a monumental day which is the 40th anniversary of me being a published author. Have a wonderful holiday season surrounded by those you love and treasure most.

Debbie Macomber

PROLOGUE

The Christmas party for Stafford Insurance had been a huge success. Lindsay Calhoun had poured her heart into organizing and planning the gathering and her hard work had paid off. She basked in the praise she'd received from her co-workers as they filed out the door. Everyone told her they'd had a great time.

Well, almost everyone.

Jack Taylor was the exception.

Lindsay wasn't surprised. She wasn't even sure why he'd bothered to show up. He'd refused to participate in the icebreakers or any of the games. He'd sat back with his arms crossed and that bored expression, as if he'd rather be anywhere else.

A few snow flurries had started to fall when everyone had first arrived. As the evening progressed, the snow had started to fall in earnest. Before anyone took notice, two to three inches had accumulated in the parking lot. When Janice from Claims had announced that a winter storm advisory had been posted, the room had cleared quickly, but Lindsay had noticed Jack heading out the door even before Janice's announcement.

A couple of Lindsay's friends had tarried long enough to ask if she needed any help with cleanup. Almost before she could assure Stephanie and Alice that she'd be fine, they had already been on their way to the parking lot. Ah, well, Lindsay couldn't really blame them. Growing up in eastern Washington, she was used to driving in winter conditions. Not so for those in the western half of the state. Seattle practically closed down if there was more than a few inches of snow.

There wasn't that much to do other than gather up leftovers and take down the decorations. She'd be on her way soon enough. Like the others, she was eager to get home, put her feet up and relax wrapped in a warm afghan. As she moved about the space, the lack of sound was a stark contrast to the friendly conversations earlier.

She headed to the kitchen to empty the punch bowl when she heard the door open. Wondering who it might be, she turned to look—and froze.

It was Jack.

Her gaze clashed with his. "Why did everyone leave in such a hurry?" he asked.

"You didn't hear?"

"Hear what?"

"There's a winter advisory, and several more inches of snow are due to arrive overnight," she explained, doing her best to ignore him while she worked.

"Anyone who took the time to look outside would see this storm isn't letting up anytime soon." Jack snorted, as if those who'd attended the party should have realized it much sooner.

"We can't all be as brilliant as you," she snapped.

He ignored her comment. "Why are you still here?"

"Cleanup," she said, as she piled the leftover sandwiches onto one plate. There were only a few left, which told her she hadn't overordered.

"You mean to say no one offered to help?"

When it came to Jack and his attitude, her tongue had teeth marks from all of the times she'd bitten back an angry reply. She'd tried with him, she really had, but to no avail.

"Yes, of course I had offers to help," she said, feeling defensive of her friends, "but I didn't want to delay anyone. As you can see, there's not that much to do. I don't suppose you're here to carry out the garbage?"

Jack shook his head. "Sounds to me like you have a martyr complex."

Lindsay glared at him. It would be easy to tell Jack Taylor exactly what she thought of him. Not that it was likely to do any good. "Whatever."

"You don't like me, do you?" he asked.

She pretended she hadn't heard that. "Seeing you didn't come back to help, exactly why are you here?"

"I can't find my car keys," he grumbled, his frustration evident in each word. "They must be here. I spent about several minutes digging through the snow all around my car. Figured they must've fallen. No luck. So they have to be here. . ."

"I haven't seen them," she said, as she tossed the empty wine bottles in the recycle bin.

"I'll check the men's room. That's the only place I can think where they might be." He headed in that direction.

If Jack was anyone else, Lindsay would make a point of helping him search. She felt mildly guilty but not enough to act.

Scowling, he returned a few minutes later.

"Find them?"

"No," he muttered with an irritated sigh. "It was those ridiculous games you dreamed up."

"Are you blaming *me* for your lost keys?" The man was unbelievable, a piece of work. "Might I remind you that you escaped into the men's room rather than participate?"

"Forgive me if I'm not into childish games. They were ridiculous."

Arms akimbo, Lindsay faced him. "You know, you might actually have enjoyed yourself if you'd taken part with everyone else. It seems sulking away the evening didn't appear to be as entertaining as you would've liked."

Splaying his fingers through his hair, he walked around the room. "I'll be out of here as soon as I find my keys."

Jack walked over to the table where he'd first sat and checked below. At the second table, he found his keys. "Found 'em," he said, and made a beeline for the front door.

"Good." Then, feeling she should be the bigger person, she added in a pleasant tone, "Despite everything, I hope you have a Merry Christmas, Jack."

He snickered, as if to say she was asking the impossible.

All at once, the lights went out and the room went dark.

"What just happened?" she asked, although it was obvious there'd been a power outage.

The room was as dark as midnight. Charcoal black. Deep cave dark.

Jack toppled over a chair, which made a clanging sound that caused Lindsay to gasp.

"It's only a chair," he said.

"Right." They needed to leave, and the sooner the better.

She'd have to return in the morning to finish up. No way could she do anything in the dark.

Before Jack could respond, a loud clicking sound came from the area of the front door.

"What was that?" she asked.

Jack blindly made his way toward the glass double-door entrance. Groaning, he turned, and in the dim light bouncing off the snow, he announced, "The door's locked."

"No, it isn't," she insisted. "It must be stuck. You just aren't pushing hard enough."

"Feel free to try yourself," he returned and stepped back.

Certain he was wrong, Lindsay found her way to where he

stood. Pushing, her shoulder against the glass, she shoved with all her strength. The door refused to budge. "It's locked," she said, doing her best to hide her dismay.

They were locked inside. They were alone. Lindsay was trapped with the last person on earth she would have chosen to spend time with.

Here she was stuck with Jack.

CHAPTER 1

*L*indsay logged onto her company's weekly Monday Zoom call, as she had every week since the team started working remotely. Zoom calls had become the norm for the small, independent insurance agency where she worked as the bookkeeper, and the physical office had closed the last day of November.

Lindsay found it less than satisfying. She much preferred it when the team had been able to meet in the office. As a people person, she didn't look forward to being cooped up inside her apartment day in and day out. When Brad, the agency's owner, had offered the choice of keeping the office open or working remotely, the vote had been almost evenly split. The deciding vote had been Jack Taylor's. Naturally, he chose to work remotely, and his vote had been the tiebreaker.

On her screen, Brad Stafford, reviewed the week, asking each department to check in with a report. Stephanie, the operations director, went first.

Lindsay was pleased to note that her fellow team members were in the Yuletide spirit; they had each decorated their Zoom backgrounds with scenes of Christmas and winter. Everyone, that is, except Jack, who'd made it known he wasn't a fan of the holiday.

Lindsay was anxious for her turn to report, since she'd spent copious amounts of personal time arranging the staff Christmas party, which was planned for later in the month. Because she worked in Accounting, she'd let it slip earlier that Brad would hand out their Christmas bonus checks at the party. This, she felt, was sure to guarantee full participation.

When asked, Lindsay gave her financial report.

"Can you update us on the party?" Brad asked. His tie featured a lighted Christmas tree that blinked as he spoke.

"I can," she said, leaning forward in her enthusiasm. "I was lucky enough to find a great location in an old bank. It's perfect for what we need even if it's in the south end of Seattle, and was recently updated with a kitchen and new flooring. The building is new on the market, which is why I was able to rent it at this late date."

"How far south?" Jack asked. He'd shown zero interest in the party. He rarely said anything on these calls, simply gave his report in a clear, precise way, limiting his words. She'd noticed he wore his long hair down for the Zoom call, rather than in a man bun. She tended to think of him as a recluse.

"It's not that far-near Auburn. I realize it's a bit out of the way, but well worth the travel time," she said, not bothering to hide her excitement. "You'll agree once you see for yourself." She didn't mention that she'd had to scramble after Brad announced they weren't renewing the lease. Before 2020, the holiday party had always been held at the office itself. Nor did she remind the others that she was working with a limited budget. "We have the building from six until nine. In addition to renting the hall for the night, I've placed the food orders."

"Did you find a gluten-free option?" Stephanie asked.

"I did," Lindsay assured her. She'd been shocked when several of the team had sought her out to make sure she'd be able to satisfy their specific food needs and preferences. "I've also ordered vegan and vegetarian options, and those of you who are lactose intolerant, I can assure you all the drinks will be dairy-free."

"What about those of us who are carnivores?" Jack asked with a snicker. He sat with his arms crossed, making sure everyone knew his feelings about the party.

When Brad had first suggested the idea, Jack had been the only staff member who claimed he wasn't interested. When Brad had asked for a volunteer to organize the event and Lindsay had been quick to offer, Jack had asked, "Why would you do that? Don't you already have enough to do?"

She had replied with the truth. "I happen to love Christmas."

Once again, Jack had scoffed. "God save us from little elves."

Lindsay remembered when she'd first met Jack. He'd only been working as the Tech expert for Stafford Insurance Agency a couple of weeks. Jack had his own cubicle, and other than break times, he rarely ventured out, so she hadn't gotten to know him the way she had many of the others. Shortly after he'd been hired, he'd stopped by her desk and requested that his paycheck be deposited to a different bank. The exchange had lasted less than a minute. She'd been curious about him, mostly because he was so private. As Jack had turned to leave, Lindsay had stopped him.

"A few of us get together Fridays after work for a beer. How about joining us?"

"No, thanks."

"Why not? It's fun and—"

"Not interested," he said before she could finish. "Why are you persisting?"

Stunned at his attitude, she had stared up at him, hardly knowing what to say. "No reason other than I was hoping to get to know you better."

"Why? I thought we were here to work, not socialize?"

Lindsay had bristled. "I do my job."

"And I do mine, and that's all you need to know about me."

"Right."

Following that short but rather uncomfortable conversation, they'd only spoken in passing, always briefly, as if Jack had better things to do than chat with her. He wasn't rude or confrontational; he was simply there to do his job. To his credit, he did it well and was available when needed.

Lately though, ever since the mention of the Christmas party, Jack had been in a mood—grouchy and negative. On the Zoom call, Lindsay stiffened at his lack of enthusiasm at every mention of the party.

"To answer your question, Jack, you needn't worry. I promise there'll be plenty to satisfy the *carnivores* among us."

"It looks like you've put a lot of effort into this," Stephanie said, clearly trying to defuse the tension. "And I, for one, want you to know how much I appreciate it."

"Hear, hear," came a chorus of replies.

Stephanie's gratitude helped smooth Lindsay's ruffled feathers.

"This gathering is important," Brad said, before Jack could comment again, "because a couple of you were hired on after the move and have yet to meet in person. As far as I'm concerned, there's no better way for us all to get to know each than attending this party, which we can do thanks to Lindsay."

Everyone but Jack seemed to agree. "Wouldn't it have been better to arrange this party during the summer?" he asked.

"Good idea, Jack. We'll plan another gathering in July," Brad concurred. "But since we've already arranged this one, it's my sincere hope that everyone will make an effort to attend." He seemed to be speaking directly to Jack.

That was Lindsay's hope, too, although she wouldn't mind if Jack decided to bow out.

"Do you need help?" Stephanie offered.

"Thanks, Steph, but I've got everything under control." By nature, Lindsay was an organizer, a trait she'd inherited from her father, along with her dark hair and rich chocolate-brown eyes. Her pert nose was from her mother.

"How long is this party supposed to last?" Jack asked with the clear indication that the sooner it was over the better.

"Like I said, we have the hall between six and nine. I have a few icebreaker games planned. I thought we could eat after, and then visit and get to know each other better."

"Games," Jack groaned. "What is this? Junior High?"

"Jack," Collin, one of the underwriters, snapped. "Your attitude isn't helping."

"Yeah.," This came from Janice, who worked in Claims.

"Jack, we can discuss this later," Brad said, as if he, too, appeared to be losing patience.

"If you don't want to attend, that isn't a problem," Lindsay chimed in.

"Let Brad deal with Jack," Stephanie advised.

"Okay, okay," Brad said. "Jack will go to the party, won't you, son?"

Lindsay wasn't sure anyone else noticed the way Jack bristled when Brad referred to him as *son*. She did, though.

Jack shrugged. "Whatever."

"I hope you do," Lindsay encouraged. "The icebreaker games I found online are going to be a lot of fun."

From the way Jack's mouth tightened, Lindsay could see he wasn't convinced.

After the call, Lindsay tried to work, but her mind continued to drift back to Jack and his attitude. She didn't know what it was about him that intrigued her—and not in a positive way. But she knew it wasn't just her. Jack was a loner. He hadn't tried to get to know any of the other team members, either. He kept to himself, ate his lunch at his desk and worked alone.

Lindsay got up, wandered around her home office, made herself a cup of coffee, then returned to her computer.

Try as she might, she still couldn't stop thinking about Jack.

CHAPTER 2

Following the Zoom call, Lindsay tried to work, but she couldn't focus. She kept thinking about Jack and his attitude. She got up from her desk again, roamed around the house, made herself another cup of coffee and returned once more to her computer. Her mind drifted back to the week of the move from the office. She'd worked hard getting everything ready for the transition and then lent a helping hand to a few of her colleagues. For the most part, everything had gone smoothly. Everyone was working extra hours.

With only a few days left before she'd be moving her workstation to her apartment, Lindsay's computer had crashed. It had been the worst possible time. Lindsay had tried everything she knew to bring it back to life without success. She had no option but to seek out Jack, the group's tech expert. To her dismay, he'd already left.

"Where's Jack?' Lindsay had asked Brad.

"He had an appointment this afternoon." He must have heard the panic in her voice. "Computer problems?"

"Big time."

"Leave him a note."

"Okay."

She 'd done as Brad suggested and eagerly watched for Jack's return, hoping that whatever had taken him away from the office wouldn't keep him too long. By closing time, he still wasn't back. Convinced she'd likely go another day without her computer, Lindsay had headed home. She hadn't slept much that night, tossing and fretting, fearing she might not be able to get payroll out on time.

To her surprise, the following morning she'd found her computer working again, with a scribbled note from Jack that read: *Up and running.* Finding his note first thing that morning had been a huge relief. Because she'd lost an entire day's work and had to do payroll, she'd been at her computer all day. Although she'd intended to thank him, she hadn't gotten a chance before Jack left the office. She could only imagine how long he'd worked or how late he'd stayed to get her up and running again. And so that night, she'd baked cookies. Her grandmother's recipe for chocolate chip cookies with walnuts.

The next day, she'd delivered them to his desk with a thank-you note. It surprised her when she didn't hear anything back from him. She'd hoped giving him the cookies would open a line of communication between them. It hadn't, and that had disappointed her. Still, busy as they were with the move, she could accept his lack of response. No need to dwell on it, she'd told herself. Jack wasn't obligated to thank her or anything. He was the one who'd helped her out.

On their last day in the office, Lindsay had finished getting everything loaded into her vehicle. Stephanie had tuned the radio to the all-Christmas station, but the cheerful sounds of "Jingle Bells" couldn't change the lonely mood of the empty space. Nearly everyone had already left. Jack had stood outside his cubicle, looking distracted. It'd been a while since she'd seen him in person, and she hadn't remembered how tall he was. He was easily over six feet.

"Anything I can do?" she'd asked. She'd helped both Janice and Stephanie, her two best friends from the agency, load up their cars earlier.

Instead of answering, Jack had appeared to be studying her. "Are you always this cheerful?"

What an odd question. It had seemed like a joke until she realized he was serious. "Mostly, yes. Does that bother you?"

His gaze had narrowed. "If you must know, I could do with a little less Mary Sunshine."

His words had stung, and she'd tried again, making light of his comment. "Oh, come on, Jack, loosen up. You got your wish—we're letting go of the office. Other than the Christmas party, we're not likely to see each other in person again."

He had snorted softly. "I should be so lucky."

Now she was offended. He was being a jerk. "Hey, that was unnecessary. I was only trying to be helpful."

He had stuffed the tips of his fingers in his jeans pockets and released a rugged sigh. "You're right. I'm not in the best mood and I don't need to be taking it out on you."

He'd apologized—well, sort of—which had surprised her. "Anything you want to talk about?"

"No." His response had been quick and to the point. He'd been as closed off as ever.

She had raised both hands as though surrendering. "Just asking."

"Asked and answered." He had avoided meeting her gaze, silently letting her know he would prefer that she leave.

"All righty then, seeing that you'd clearly prefer me to move along, I'll go." Then, because he'd irked her, she had added, "And just so you know, you're permanently off my homemade cookie list."

Having made her feelings known, she'd started toward the

front of the office only to hear him mumble behind her. It had taken her a moment to make out his words: "Darn, I should've kept my mouth shut."

As Lindsay had left the office, she couldn't keep the smile off her face.

CHAPTER 3

The day of the party, Lindsay woke up excited about the evening ahead. She intended to finish the last of her errands and arrive at the rented hall well before starting time.

While on the road, Lindsay called her mother to update her on how her day was going. "I want to make this Christmas party something special," she said, speaking through the Bluetooth in her vehicle. "Well, maybe not for Jack Taylor, the Grinch personified!"

"Lindsay, be kind. There might well be a reason he's such a Jack Frost."

"Good one, Mom!"

"But you agree?"

"Mostly," Lindsay murmured. Jack was Jack. He'd been a constant thorn in her side for weeks. The fact that he'd rejected every effort she'd made to be friends rankled her. The only aspect of this party that worried her was Jack. He would likely put a damper on the entire evening. In fact, she suspected that was his intention.

"He's really gotten under your skin, hasn't he?" her mother asked, although it was more of a comment than a question.

"He has," she confessed. "If you met him, you'd know what I mean. Being around him is a downer. I'm afraid he's going to ruin everything, and I've worked so hard to make tonight perfect."

"Lindsay, my goodness, listen to yourself. You're making assumptions about him. He might just surprise you."

"I doubt it," she muttered. She had half a mind to tell her mother Jack would show up simply to spite her. "Did I tell you that he called me Mary Sunshine?" She grimaced every time she thought about it. "The way he said it suggested being around me was like falling into a sickeningly sweet jar of honey."

"Did you consider that might have been a compliment?"

"Not likely." Her mother had always been one to believe the best of others. "It was a dig and not one I'm eager to forget or forgive."

"Oh, Lindsay . . ."

"I'm sorry, Mom, I didn't mean to dump on you, especially when you and Dad are ready to leave on your cruise."

"No worries. I'm happy to listen to your frustrations. A word of advice, though. Don't be so quick to judge Jack."

She'd try. "I'll do my best," she promised.

"Did you bake the fruitcake recipe I emailed?" her mother asked in a blatant effort to change the subject. "You know it's been in the family for generations and a family favorite. I'm sure your coworkers will want the recipe but please don't share it."

Her mother enjoyed the hard-as-a-rock fruitcake but no one else in the family did, something her mother chose to ignore. Every holiday, Lindsay did her best to disguise how much she disliked that particular tradition. She wasn't the only one, either. It had become something of a family conspiracy to pretend to enjoy the fruitcake while finding clever ways to dispose of it.

"Sorry, Mom, no time. Maybe next year." She suspected that if her coworkers knew, they would forever thank her for sparing them.

"What did you think of my ideas for the party games?"

"Pinning the hat on Santa while blindfolded?" Lindsay murmured. Her mother had only tried to help. "That's more a game for kids, don't you think? I appreciate the suggestion, though."

"I should've known you'd have everything under control. You're so much like your father. He's got an itinerary for every day of our Christmas cruise planned."

"Of course, he does," Lindsay said with a smile. Her parents were taking their first cruise, which coincided with Christmas and their thirtieth wedding anniversary. Lindsay would miss spending Christmas with her parents, but she couldn't begrudge them this long-anticipated trip.

"You sure you don't want to join Kelly and John for the holidays?" her mother asked for the umpteenth time.

"Mom, please, we've already been through this. Kelly is spending Christmas with John's family. My sister doesn't need me tagging along. I'll be fine. Now stop feeling guilty, I'm going to have a perfectly wonderful Christmas on my own."

"Oh, honey, are you sure?"

"I'm positive. In fact, I've lined up several projects I've been wanting to do and never seem to have time for."

"Bake a fruitcake, okay?"

"Mom!" No way was she up for that.

"It will remind you of home."

"Don't be silly," Lindsay said with a laugh. "I'll come visit after the first of the year when you're back from your cruise and you can share all the details. We'll have our own Christmas then."

"Okay," her mother agreed, although she continued to sound both guilty and excited at once. "Call me after the party. I want to know how everything turns out."

"Will do," Lindsay promised and disconnected.

. . .

THE TALK about the party games reminded Lindsay of the joke gifts she'd arranged. She was rather pleased with her ideas. She had a water bottle with a sign that claimed it was a melted snowman. Another was several cotton balls in plastic wrap that she'd labeled a Pet Cloud. Her favorite was a plastic eye attached to a pad of paper, which she called an iPad. Those were all for fun. She'd had several less cheesy prizes, too, but felt her friends would enjoy the joke ones just as much.

On the drive out to Auburn where she'd rented the hall, she picked up the food. There hadn't been enough in the budget to have the event catered, which meant she had to collect each order herself. And because there were several dietary preferences and needs, she was obliged to make three separate stops. The sky was overcast, and freezing temperatures were predicted overnight with a chance of snow. She could only hope that Jack would use the weather as an excuse not to attend the party.

He'd complained that the location was outside Seattle, although no one else seemed to mind. But then, Jack complained about everything. It wasn't as if there was an abundance of spaces available, taking into account that she had a limited budget.

She'd visited the converted bank building earlier in the month and thought it was perfect. The structure had been built in the mid-1950s with polished wood molding giving it a homey appeal. The oak tables and chairs seemed original and made stepping into the building feel like traveling back in time. The interior areas had been opened up so that the light from the windows filled the entire hall. The event space was geared toward small gatherings, such as theirs. Part of the renovation had included a new kitchen with convenient access to the main part of the room.

Lindsay had been assured the door would be unlocked when she arrived, and it was. After she'd unloaded all the food and decorations, she set about making the hall as festive as possible. She adorned tables with sprigs of holly, full of bright red berries, centering a silver candle on each table. She placed a wreath on the far wall and strung garlands of tinsel around the windows.

As she worked, she chatted on the phone with her best friend, Shelly. They'd met in fifth grade and been besties ever since. Shelly was recently married and had invited Lindsay to spend Christmas with her and Henry. No way was she going to crash her friend's first Christmas as a married woman!

"It's going to be a terrific party," Shelly said, with all the assurance of a close friend. "You don't have a thing to worry about."

"That's my hope anyway. Although I can't help fretting a bit." Lindsay said.

"Because of Mr. Grinch, you mean."

Lindsay clearly had mentioned Jack more often than she'd realized. Shelly had just asked about him, and she'd brought Jack up with her mom earlier. She had to admit he'd been on her mind far more than the disagreeable party pooper warranted. "The weather report says we might get snow."

"Sounds like Jack would use that as an excuse not to attend."

"I was thinking the same thing," Lindsay returned. She'd known Shelly so long their thoughts often echoed each other's. Lindsay could only hope. She suspected Brad had made sure Jack understood his attendance was expected, if not required.

"Don't let one curmudgeon get you down," Shelly advised.

"I won't." It would be hard, though.

"And call me tomorrow and update me on how everything went."

"Okay, I will." By the time she'd finished, it was almost five o'clock. It wouldn't be long before everyone arrived. Lindsay was pleased with her decorating efforts. The hall was festive-looking, and she had the evening under control. All of her preparation and hard work was about to pay off.

Stephanie and Collin were the first to arrive. They'd carpooled, as they lived relatively close to each other. Lindsay had set up a table for the Secret Santa gift exchange and they both placed their wrapped packages on the table.

Once Stephanie hung up her winter coat on the rack close to the door, she paused, looked about the room and nodded. "Wow, Lindsay, you've done a great job!"

"Thanks." She felt herself blush with pleasure.

Although familiar with her fellow team members, Lindsay had placed name tags, printed with holly and berries along the edges, on a table by the coat rack. While she was good at remembering names, she wasn't sure others were.

Close to six, Brad turned up wearing a Santa hat. "Ho, ho, ho!" he called out as he entered. He wore the same Christmas-tree tie with blinking lights he'd had on during every December Zoom meeting. A cheer rose, and Lindsay was fairly certain it was because her employer had tossed a small red bag over his shoulder, which she knew contained the Christmas bonus checks.

To her disappointment, Jack Taylor arrived several minutes after six, and Lindsay groaned inwardly. Guess the threat of snow wasn't enough to keep him away. He wore his hair in a man bun and dressed in a black leather jacket and jeans. She couldn't help wondering if he had a sleeve of tattoos down his arms. He'd worn a long-sleeved shirt every time she'd seen him prior to the party. It wouldn't surprise her if he had multiple tattoos. He seemed the type, giving off bad-boy vibes. Bad boy, bad attitude, to complete his persona. And, of course, he was the one team member who'd declined to take part in the Secret Santa activities.

Standing in front of the room, Lindsay waited until everyone had found a chair at one of the tables. Normally, she disliked being the center of attention, but she was the one who'd volunteered and as such acted as host.

"Now that everyone's arrived," Lindsay said, nervously rubbing her palms together, "I thought it would be fun to play a few games as icebreakers. We all know each other in a limited way, and for those of you who joined us most recently, all you've seen are our faces during Zoom meetings. I chose these games as a way for us to connect outside of the office, more as friends than coworkers."

The tables were divided evenly with six people at each of the four tables. Brad sat with the two highest-ranking insurance agents, plus Stephanie, Collin and Jack.

"For the first game, I want everyone to go around and share a favorite Christmas memory."

Jack groaned loudly enough for everyone to hear. Lindsay chose to ignore him. "If not a memory, then a special gift you've received." She eyed Jack, wondering if that would appease him.

There was lots of chatter, and everything seemed to be going well, with one exception. Jack. Why was she surprised? He leaned back in his chair with his arms crossed over his chest. His body language said everything. No way was he willing to participate.

Lindsay had tried hard to find games that would help create a sense of community. She moved people from table to table, making sure there was lots of interaction and mingling.

It bothered her that she'd had let Jack unsettle her. She had to accept that nothing she said or did was going to make a bit of difference to his attitude. Deciding to ignore him, she sat down at one of the tables herself and joined in on the conversation. She told the story of how as an eight-year-old, all she'd wanted for Christmas was a pony. No way could her parents afford a horse. Instead, she'd gotten a gift certificate for riding lessons, which she'd loved, and rode for several years. It was her best Christmas gift by far. Even now she made a point of riding whenever she was home.

She listened while the others shared their memories of the holidays and was pleased with how well everything seemed to be going. As best she could, she ignored Jack Taylor.

CHAPTER 4

*T*he last icebreaker was called the marshmallow game, and it was one that required teamwork and coordination. Each table was given twenty strands of dry spaghetti and one marshmallow. The idea was to form a Christmas tree with the spaghetti and place the marshmallow on top. The assignment wasn't as easy as it sounded. The first team to manage the task got the prize: an Advent wine sampler of 24 mini-bottles that could be divided equally among the six participants.

Lindsay pitied the team members at the table where Jack sat. When she explained the objective of the game, she watched him roll his eyes. While his tablemates tackled the project, Jack disappeared into the restroom, which she guessed was another escape tactic.

When he returned, he lingered in the back of the room, close to the kitchen, where Lindsay was busy carrying the platters of sandwiches, salads, and desserts from the giant refrigerator.

"Aren't you going to join your team?" she asked, hoping to encourage him.

He snorted, as though she'd said something amusing.

Placing her hands on her hips, she glared at him. "I don't know why you came when it's clear you don't want to be here."

Jack agreed. "You got that right. This is the last place I want to be."

"Then why come?"

He shrugged. "Brad told me it was mandatory."

Brad must have hoped that if he could get Jack to the party, he'd open up a bit more and socialize. Clearly that ploy hadn't worked.

"Hey," he said coming into the kitchen. "Let me help with those food trays."

His offer came as a pleasant surprise until she realized this was his way of avoiding those involved in the table games.

"Thanks, but no thanks," she said ever so sweetly. She enjoyed thwarting him. "I've got this."

He shrugged again. "Your choice."

A cheer rose in the background. Lindsay glanced into the main part of the space to find the table that had managed to get the spaghetti into the shape of a tree exchanging high fives in triumph. It was the receptionist and office assistance group, which pleased Lindsay as they were often underappreciated.

Following the games, Lindsay announced that the food was ready. "I have everything labeled, so come and help yourselves."

"I'll open some more bottles of wine," Brad offered.

It wasn't long before the wine and punch flowed freely. Lindsay sat back, savoring the laughter and camaraderie that filled the room. Several people toured the old bank and walked inside the safe. Sheila, one of the insurance agents, mentioned a restaurant in Denver where she had dinner in an old bank.

Seeing how the team members interacted with each other, Lindsay knew all her efforts had been worthwhile. Enjoying the conversation and laughter, she watched as acquaintances became friends. This was exactly what she'd hoped would happen.

Brad came to stand next to her and patted her on the back. "You did a wonderful job, Lindsay."

"Thank you." This party meant a great deal to her, especially since she wouldn't be sharing Christmas with her family this year.

"I notice you've been busy this entire evening. Did you have time to eat something yourself?"

"I ate earlier." She'd sampled a couple of the tri-cut sandwiches before the team arrived, but she hadn't eaten anything since. For now, she was being fed by the praise and appreciation of her coworkers.

As the party wound down, Brad handed out the Christmas bonuses. Lindsay expected everyone to leave once they had the check. The only person she saw walk out the door the minute he had his was Jack.

"Hey," Janice from Claims called out. "Anyone look outside recently?"

Several of the staff glanced toward the windows. "Oh, goodness," Janice continued with a worried frown, looking down at her phone. "There's a winter storm advisory. Looks like we're in for one heck of a storm."

That was all it took for everyone to grab their hats and coats and race for the door.

CHAPTER 5

*A*fter everyone had left, and Jack had returned to search for his car keys, it wasn't long before they lost power and the dreaded sound of the front door lock echoed through the room.

As much as Lindsay wanted Jack to be wrong, the front door refused to budge despite both their efforts. As best they could figure, the mechanism must be tied to the power. Lindsay recalled a friend who worked at a bank explaining that the doors leading into the building were set up to lock. It appeared that the owners of the old bank hadn't changed the system.

"It'll probably only take a few minutes before the electricity's restored," she said, more to reassure herself than out of any confidence. Lindsay was doing her best not to panic, but this wasn't good. In fact, it was downright awful. The thought of being trapped with him for any length of time made her groan inwardly. Only heaven knew how long it would take before they were discovered. Knowing Jack, he'd make any extended period of time trapped in the same room utterly miserable for them both. He'd complain and harp on about it and likely find a way to blame her for this fiasco.

"All right," she said, taking in a slow, calming breath as she rubbed her open palms together, thinking out loud. "There's no need to overreact. All we need to do is call someone for help."

"Right."

"You call," she suggested. Her phone was on life support. She'd been calling and texting all day.

"Why me?"

"Why *not* you?" she retorted.

"I can't. My phone's in the car."

Lindsay placed both hands on top of her head. "No, no, no! This can't be happening!"

"What's the big deal? Use *your* phone."

She withdrew it from her pocket and showed him the barely visible red line, revealing what little power remained.

He reached for her phone and frowned. "You likely have enough juice to make at least one call."

That was optimistic at best. "If so, we need to be sure whoever we reach will be able to help."

"Nine-one-one?" Jack suggested.

"I . . . I don't know if they'd consider this an emergency. We aren't the only ones without power. With the storm, first responders are going to get far more important calls than ours. It shouldn't take long for the power to return." She could only hope she was right.

"Calling nine-one-one is our best bet, although I get your point."

"I don't think it would work anyway. If we did call and explain, they'll likely call back to confirm this isn't a prank and my phone will be dead."

Jack glared up at the ceiling and released a groan. "You're probably right. The one time I needed nine-one-one, the operator asked me about twenty questions, keeping me on the phone for five minutes or more."

"The operator will think I've hung up."

They were both silent for several minutes, weighing their options.

"What about Brad?" he finally suggested.

Lindsay quickly discarded the idea. "I don't have Brad's personal number, do you?"

"No," he admitted.

"We need to decide while I still have power. We have one chance and only one—if that. We have to reach someone who'll be able to get us out of here."

"Right," he agreed. He didn't look any happier than she did.

"I think our best bet is the leasing agency," Lindsay said. "Someone must have a key. Right?" She looked to Jack for assurance that her thinking made sense.

"We can only hope."

"This likely isn't the first time this has happened," she added. Lindsay chewed on her upper lip, as she remembered the agent explaining that the old bank building had a locking factor tied to the front door. He'd mentioned this fact, she now assumed this wasn't the first time someone had gotten locked inside. It made sense that the rental agency would have staff on duty.

"Okay, go for it."

Lindsay got her purse and pulled out the rental agreement. She spread the paperwork across the top of the table as if it were something precious like a page from the first edition of the Gutenberg Bible.

Inhaling, she pulled out a chair and sat down. Jack sat next to her. Her phone's thin sliver of red had all but disappeared.

With her heart in her throat, Lindsay punched out the number and held her breath as the phone rang five times before a tinny voice responded. *"We're sorry to miss your call. Please try again during our office hours, Monday through Saturday, from eight to five. If you want to leave a message . . ."*

Her phone powered down and died.

Jack laid his head on the table and groaned. "So much for that."

"Stupid, stupid, stupid. I should've realized—"

"Stop it, Lindsay," he snapped. "This isn't your fault. We're two intelligent people, so we should be able to figure a way out of here."

"This is bad, really bad . . ."

"Come on, think. Haven't you ever heard the saying, *Where there's a will, there's a way*? All we need to do is find the way, because I, for one, have no desire to be trapped here for any length of time."

"Me, neither," she said, thinking how comfortable and welcome her bed would be after such a long, tiring day.

"We'll sort it out," Jack said and squeezed her hand.

Lindsay hadn't expected him to be this reassuring or understanding.

"Maybe there's a landline here!" she suggested. It made sense. Especially if this had happened before. She hadn't seen one, but that didn't mean there wasn't one. The most likely location was the kitchen.

"Good idea," Jack said. With hope and enthusiasm, they made their way into the other room, fumbling through the dark.

Jack located a flashlight in one of the drawers, which allowed them to make a thorough search--the walls, the drawers, every conceivable place a phone might be.

No landline anywhere.

"What's with these people," Jack grumbled. "The least they could do is have a phone."

Lindsay was in full agreement, although she assumed that others who were trapped here would likely be able to use their own devices. Just their luck that wasn't the case for them.

Silence settled again as they weighed their options. They walked carefully back to the table and took a seat.

Lindsay wasn't full of ideas, but she did have one. "We could break a window and risk the possibility of getting cut or being charged with a crime."

"There are mitigating circumstances," Jack said. "But I don't think Brad would be pleased with you if we had to pay for the replacement."

"You're right."

He chuckled. "We could start a fire."

"And risk dying from smoke inhalation," Lindsay said. His idea wasn't any better than hers.

"Yeah, that wasn't my most brilliant suggestion."

"Why don't we wait for an hour or so and see what happens. Surely the power company's been called by now and is working on solving the problem," Lindsay said.

Jack straightened. "Good idea. What about your husband? Will he worry if you aren't home soon?"

"I'm not married."

"Your roommate?"

She shook her head. "I live alone. You?"

"The same." Jack set the flashlight on the table closest to where they sat, giving them muted light.

Folding her arms on the table, Lindsay mulled over their situation. "I don't think we have any other choice but to wait it out. There's no need to panic, right?"

"Right." But Jack didn't sound convinced. "Is anyone else likely to check on us?" he added. "Who's going to miss us?"

"My mother," Lindsay said. "I promised I'd call after the party to tell her how everything went. If she doesn't hear from me and can't reach me, she might call one of my friends."

"You seriously think that's a possibility?"

He was right; that was a stretch. It wasn't likely her mom expected to hear from her until morning. "Not really. What about you? Is there anyone who would miss you?"

"Hardly."

Jack got up from the table. "I don't suppose there's any wine left? If we're going to be stuck here, we might as well make ourselves comfortable."

"There were a couple half-full bottles in the kitchen."

Using the flashlight, Jack made his way there and returned with a bottle and two cups.

"It seems wrong to drink good wine out of a paper cup," Lindsay commented.

Jack laughed. "Hey, I didn't see any glasses. So, any port in a storm, right?"

She smiled, remembering that she'd piled all the glasses in the dishwasher. Jack studied the label. "Organic Chardonnay. Excellent choice."

"Thanks." They toasted each other and Lindsay took a sip. She hadn't indulged during the party, and she had to admit the wine was a good idea.

They didn't speak, both caught in their own thoughts, she suspected.

The second glass of wine, a Cabernet, loosened her up. "Do you mind if I ask you something?"

He waved his hand in her direction. "Have at it."

"Are you a recluse?"

He snorted, seeming shocked at the question. "Me a recluse? Nope."

"You're so . . ." She struggled to find the right word. "Unless you were complaining about the party, you didn't say much during our Zoom meetings. And . . . you seem reluctant to engage with the team."

"So what?"

"You seem, you know, closed off." She didn't mention the few times she'd reached out a hand of friendship to him and been soundly rejected. No need to bring that up.

"What if I am? I do my job and solve problems when I need to. What else do you want?"

"I don't know," she said, mulling over what had prompted the question. "I shouldn't have said anything."

"I'm curious why you asked."

She thought about it for a moment, then said. "I'm not sure. I guess it's because you seem so . . ."

"Unfriendly," he supplied, finishing the thought for her.

"More negative, I guess. That's the vibe I get from you, especially when it came to the party."

"Christmas isn't my thing," he said. "Now can I ask you a question?"

"Have at it," she said, parroting his earlier words.

"You say you're single."

"I am, as are you." She held up her wine cup and clicked the edge of his.

"Is there anyone special in your life?"

She smiled at the question. It indicated that he was curious about her, which she found interesting, because she felt the same about him.

"You mean like a significant other?" she asked.

He nodded.

"Nope. What about you?"

"I'm asking about you," he shot back.

After two full glasses of wine, Lindsay was feeling more than a little lightheaded.

"Don't you date?" he asked.

"Sure, off and on, but there's no one special." She waved her hand toward him. "Enough about me. Is there anyone special in your life?"

"Yeah."

"Oh." Her spirits sank. "What's her name?"

"Oscar."

Despite herself, Lindsay gulped at the surprise of it.

"And actually, it's a *he*, and he's a dog. My mom's got him tonight, thankfully."

Outraged, Lindsay slugged his shoulder while Jack laughed. "You should've seen the look on your face."

"That wasn't funny."

"Tell me something about yourself," he said next.

"I will if you will."

"Sure. But you go first. And make it something I likely wouldn't know about you." The wine appeared to have the same effect on Jack as it did Lindsay. He was more relaxed than she'd ever seen him.

"You mean that I have some obscure fetish?"

"All the better."

Lindsay snickered. "Sorry to disappoint you, Jack Taylor."

"Okay, tell me whatever you want me to think I should know about you. The less anyone else does, the better."

"Okay, don't be shocked, but I have a tattoo. I haven't even told my mother." Her mother would have a conniption if she ever learned she and Shelly had gotten identical tattoos right before Shelly's wedding. They knew their relationship was bound to change and decided to seal their friendship with a rose tattoo.

Jack's brows rose halfway to his hairline as though he found it hard to believe. "A tattoo? Where?"

She had to place it where her mother wasn't likely to see. "My hip, and I'm not showing it to you, so don't ask."

He wiggled his eyebrows playfully. "I'll show you mine if you show me yours."

"Not happening," she said, laughing as she reached for her wine and took another sip. "It doesn't surprise me that you have one, though."

"Wanna see?"

She studied him through narrowed eyes, half-suspecting he would then insist she reveal her own. "Only if you want to show it to me. But don't expect me to return the favor. "

Standing, Jack removed his jacket and pushed up the sleeve of his sweater to reveal the colorful head of an American eagle and the words "Semper Fidelis."

Now Lindsay *was* surprised. "You were a Marine."

He seemed to have trouble holding back a smile. "Once a Marine, always a Marine."

This was something she would never have guessed. Her expression must have given away her bewilderment because he asked, "Why the shocked look?"

She felt foolish for having prejudged him. "I . . . I don't know. I guess I've always viewed you as something of a rebel." The more time she spent with Jack, the more she liked him, and that was something she hadn't expected.

He grinned and she noticed how his face relaxed when he smiled. To her astonishment, she found him strikingly handsome. This was Jack, she had to remind herself. Jack *Frost*. The curmudgeon. The Grinch. Scrooge and every other Christmas villain personified. Without realizing it, she must have been staring.

"What?" Jack asked as though confused. "Is my being a Marine that much of a shock?"

"No, sorry." Embarrassed now, she got up from the table, looking for a way to change the subject. The lone package sitting on the table by the entrance was a welcome distraction. "I didn't open my secret Santa gift."

"Because you were too busy making sure everyone else was having a good time," he commented with an edge to his voice.

"You say it like it's a bad thing."

"Not implying anything," he insisted.

Lindsay collected the lone gift and unwrapped it. Her eyes lit up with delight. "Look, it's a gingerbread house. Let's assemble it." She didn't actually expect him to agree but decided to ask anyway. Before he could refuse, she added, "I mean, we don't have anything else to do. It'll help pass the time."

He walked over to where she stood and stared down at her gift. "A gingerbread house. Really?" He shook his head and while she wasn't certain in the dim light, she guessed he'd rolled his eye too.

His lack of enthusiasm was hardly unexpected. "Okay, I'll do it alone. I'll need you to hold the light, though."

He rolled his eyes. "Okay. Whatever."

Lindsay tore open the box and carefully arranged all the pieces before unfolding the instructions and reading them aloud. She set the sides in place, then began using the tube of frosting, when Jack stopped her.

"That's not right," he said. "You need to put the frosting on the pieces first to join them together, not the way you're doing it."

Caught unawares, she paused, the frosting tube in hand. "Oh." She looked at the illustration again and discovered he was right. "Thanks."

"No problem." He held the flashlight higher to give her a better view. "That help?"

"It does," she said, returning to her task.

It wasn't long before they traded places and Jack continued with the assembly. Once the gingerbread house had four walls and a roof, they needed to wait for the frosting to set before adding the embellishments. When Lindsay looked up, she saw that Jack was eating the small gumdrops that were supposed to be the tiles on the roof.

"Jack!"

"Some of my favorites. Have one."

She should be annoyed, but they'd had such a good time putting the house together, she found it impossible to care. Taking the candy out of his hand, she popped it in her mouth.

"I like the black licorice ones best."

"My favorites are the red cherry."

Jack reached into the bag and brought out all the red ones for her.

Lindsay ate them all.

They sat back down at the table and Jack turned off the flashlight. "Seeing that this is taking longer than we hoped, we should conserve the battery."

"Good idea," she agreed, although sitting in the dark with Jack felt intimate in a way it hadn't earlier.

This was by far the longest time she'd spent with him, and it had been an eye-opener. On his own, Jack was a completely different person.

"You said you thought I was a recluse," he said. "Well, I had an opinion of you, as well. Confession time."

She wasn't sure she was going to like what he had to say.

"I viewed you as something of a goodie two-shoes. An apple pie and Girl Scout cookies kind of gal. I bet you were prom queen, a member of the National Honor Society and won statewide spelling bees."

Despite her irritation, she laughed because she *had* been one of the prom queen candidates and came in first in the city-wide spelling bee in the fifth grade. And her marks were always among the best. Jack certainly had her pegged.

"I'm right, aren't I?"

She nodded. "As it happens, I did get top grades, and in Grade Five I won a spelling bee. I was in the running for prom queen in high school but didn't end up winning."

"Knew it," he said with a note of triumph. "See? You did everything I said you did."

"You make it sound like that's a bad thing." How unflattering. She crossed her arms and huffed.

"Chill, Lindsay."

She turned her head and looked away. The fact that he'd read her so accurately embarrassed her.

"My turn," he said, and poured them the last of the wine.

"I suppose you're going to tell me what a rebellious youth you were and how you got expelled from school in a Christmas prank gone awry."

"Wrong guess."

"I'm waiting," she said impatiently.

He grew solemn. "Actually, I was about to tell you why I hate Christmas."

"Okay, I'll go for it. Why do you hate Christmas?"

He leaned back in the chair and exhaled, as though he wanted to separate himself from her or from whatever he was about to tell her. "When I was in the fifth grade, my dad left my mom, my twin sisters and me on Christmas Eve."

CHAPTER 6

*J*ack was quiet and sat still for a long moment. In a matter of seconds, the entire atmosphere had changed. Minutes ago, they'd been laughing and joking while assembling the gingerbread house. Now there was a heaviness in the air and Jack seemed hesitant to continue. She heard the pain in his voice and knew the only reason he'd even mentioned his father was because they were in the dark. It was as though he'd lowered his guard and could speak freely as long as she couldn't read his expression.

Lindsay didn't know if she should say anything or not, and so, awkward as it was, she waited patiently for him to speak.

"I don't know why I'm telling you this," he said, after what felt like an eternity.

Reaching for his hand, Lindsay gently folded her fingers around his. "Please, if you'd rather not explain, then don't. It isn't necessary." Seeing how uncomfortable he was, she felt a strong urge to put him at ease.

His hand tightened around hers. "The highlight of your fifth grade was winning a spelling bee. Whereas my fifth-grade experience was one of the lowest points of my life."

"I'm sorry, Jack."

The pressure of his hand around hers tightened until it was almost painful. She wondered if this connection between them, this physical connection, was keeping him grounded in the present as he opened up about his wounds from the past.

"You jokingly suggested I got expelled from school."

Lindsay deeply regretted that remark now. "That was a mean thing to say. I apologize."

He chuckled softly. "Actually, that isn't far from the truth."

He didn't speak for several long moments. "Christmas Eve," he began, "Mom had baked my favorite gingerbread cookies, and my sisters were counting the gifts under the tree. Dad was gone a lot because of his work schedule." He paused, as though reliving that time all over again.

Wanting to fill the silence, she said, "Gingerbread cookies are one of my favorites, too."

He smirked. "I haven't eaten one since that Christmas. When I said my dad was away because of his work schedule, that was a lie. Not mine. His. He'd met someone else. Christmas Eve, he didn't come home. As you can imagine, my mother was worried sick."

"Anyone would be."

"Mom tried to hide her anxiety from me and my sisters, but young as I was, even then, I knew something was wrong. We were always allowed to open one gift on Christmas Eve, and both of my sisters were standing by the window waiting for Dad to arrive. Once he was home, we could each open our present, which by the way, was always pajamas. When he didn't show up for dinner, Mom invented some excuse and said we could go ahead with our gifts. I insisted I'd wait for Dad, and Mom let me.

"Later, she put us to bed with the promise that Santa would arrive during the night, and Dad would be there when we woke up. She sounded confident. My twin sisters, Beth and Emma, accepted her word and went to bed chatting excitedly about Santa's visit. I was old enough to know about Santa, and I knew my mother was trying hard to hide her fears with talk of Christmas and all the gifts Santa would soon deliver. But my sisters still believed, and I wasn't about to disillusion them."

"You were the oldest, then?"

"Yeah, the oldest by five years. I turned ten that October. After Beth and Emma were asleep, I snuck out of bed and listened from the hallway while my mother was on the phone. She called the hospitals and several friends in a frantic effort to find my dad."

"Did she?"

"No, he'd simply disappeared. When we woke the next morning and Dad was still gone, mom made some flimsy excuse. She did her best to make Christmas as festive as she could. The following day, we learned my dad had emptied their savings account, quit his job and left town with another woman."

"Oh Jack, how awful!" No wonder he wasn't fond of Christmas.

"My father abandoned his family, leaving us penniless. My mom's parents helped us as much as they could, but they didn't have a lot of extra themselves. I don't think they liked my dad much even before he left. Mom, who was a registered nurse, worked nights, and I remember how exhausted she was as she struggled to support us. Eventually she found a second job. I think she tried hard to keep the house, but eventually, we had to move into government housing."

Lindsay could imagine how difficult this time was for Jack's family. At ten years old, Jack had taken on a heavy load of responsibility, helping his mother and caring for his sisters while she was at work.

"Nothing was the same. We went from being a middle-class family to food stamps and free school lunches. I started acting out my anger in the classroom and was soon labeled a troublemaker."

His story explained a great deal about his prickly personality. Not knowing how best to respond, Lindsay went by instinct and leaned close to him, placing her head on his shoulder.

He gave a short, humorless laugh. "I don't talk about my dad. Not ever. I have no idea why I'm spilling my guts to you."

"It's the wine."

He seemed to agree, as he lifted his cup and took a deep drink. "You're probably right."

Every bad thought she'd entertained about him gave way to understanding and acceptance. She'd been the one to push all the festive activities in his face. How she wished she'd accepted that Jack had a reason for his attitude toward the holidays and left things alone.

"Well, whether it was the wine or being trapped here or whatever. . . I'm grateful." He'd bared his soul to her, opened his heart, and Lindsay was deeply touched.

"Why would you be grateful?" He seemed taken aback by her words.

"Because you trusted me, and I have a feeling you don't give your trust easily."

"How could I not trust you?" he joked. "You're Miss Sunshine, happy and cheerful, generous and so darn cute I sometimes wonder if you're real."

His compliment flustered her, and she touched her hair. "I'm real, all right, far *too* real. Do you want to know why this party was so important to me?"

"Sure. You love Christmas. Isn't that what you said?"

"That's true, but this year is completely different. My parents are taking a long-awaited and much-anticipated Christmas cruise. I could spend the holidays with my sister but she's going to her in-laws' home, and I'd feel out of place. My best friend invited me to join her, but this is Shelly's first year as a wife, and I don't want to intrude on her, either. So I decided I'd stay in town and have my own private Christmas. I did a bit of decorating in my apartment, but it didn't feel the same. Planning this party is my Christmas. It was something I could get excited about and know I was making the holiday more festive for others."

Scooting his chair closer to hers, Jack placed his chin on top of her head. "I get it. Beth won't be able to make it home for Christmas this year, either. She's going to Boston to meet her fiancé's family. Mom's delighted by the engagement—of course— but terribly disappointed not to see her this Christmas."

"My mom threatened to cancel the cruise because she didn't want me to spend Christmas alone. I wouldn't let her. Dad planned this months ago. It's their anniversary and their first cruise. You see, by putting my energy into organizing this party, I could stop feeling sorry for myself and do something positive."

"I'm glad you did."

"You are not," she objected, snickering softly. "You hated the very idea from the moment Brad brought it up."

"True, but it turned out well in the end, don't you think?"

"That's sweet of you to say."

He chuckled. "Listen, there's nothing sweet about me, and you shouldn't forget that."

Lindsay ignored the comment. "I still don't understand why you didn't want to attend the party. Parties are fun. You like fun, don't you?"

"Sure, but Christmas parties have a reputation. I'm grateful none of our team ended up drunk and dancing around the room with lamp shades on their heads."

Lindsay couldn't help it; she laughed. "We had a great time even without the lamp shades."

"Like I said, the evening turned out better than I'd expected."

Coming from Jack, that was high praise.

"But now we're stuck here," she said. "And from the way it looks, the electricity isn't coming back anytime soon."

He shrugged. "It's not so bad."

"Really?" She had to admit his attitude was a pleasant surprise.

"You don't agree?" he asked.

"I do, but I'll admit I had a small panic attack when I realized our situation."

He chuckled. "At least you weren't alone. You might have been terrified trapped in the dark all by yourself."

"That's certainly one positive." Another bonus was getting to know Jack better. The more they were together, the more she felt drawn to him.

Jack grew thoughtful. "I don't know how I'll feel once we're set free. I suspect I'll regret telling you about my dad."

"Do you mind me asking if you ever heard from him again?" She wanted Jack's father to have lived a miserable life. At the same time, she hoped there had been healing for his family.

"I don't mind. We did hear from my dad about ten years later. I was a Marine at the time, so I wasn't home. That was a good thing because I probably wouldn't have let him in the house. He showed up where Mom and the twins lived, claiming he wanted to apologize. From what she told me, it was all part of some twelve-step program about making amends whenever possible."

"Your mother must have been stunned after all those years."

"That's putting it mildly. Mom never remarried, and somehow my father believed she carried a torch for him all the time he was missing. He seemed convinced that, with a bit of persuasion, she'd be willing to take him back. Mom wasn't interested. She'd been fooled by him once. She wasn't about to risk her heart on him a second time. It was clear he'd hit bottom. He hung around town until he was forced to accept that she wasn't going to change her mind, then he left. We haven't heard from him since, and that's fine by me."

"Your mother must be a strong woman."

"She is. I admire her more than anyone. After my dad disappeared, she never once lost her faith, trusting God to take care of us, and believed He would supply all our needs."

Just the way Jack spoke about his mother told her how much he loved her. "The two of you are close, aren't you?"

"We are."

"I'm close to my mom, too. We talk at least twice a week."

He grinned. "Guess we do have something in common, after all."

They sat in companionable silence for several minutes. Then Lindsay's stomach growled. Embarrassed, she pressed her hands against her midsection.

"You're hungry."

"I was too busy at the party to eat," she explained. "There are a few sandwiches left. I'll grab one. Do you want anything?" she asked, and then teased him. "I believe there might be a couple of the carnivore ones on the tray."

He snickered softly. "No, thanks."

Grabbing hold of the flashlight, Lindsay got up from the table and helped herself to the leftovers. When she looked out the window, she saw that the snow was piling up faster and faster.

"Jack!" she cried, her hand flying to her mouth.

"What?" He leaped to his feet so fast he nearly knocked over his chair.

"Look how beautiful the snow is." She walked over to the window to watch. Standing by her side, Jack frowned and shook his head.

"You actually love the snow?" He said this as if she was being ridiculous.

"How can you not? It's so . . . white and pure. It doesn't happen that often in Seattle, so this is a treat, especially in December."

"Snow is nothing but a hassle," he said. "People don't know how to drive in it, and that causes pileups all along the roadways.

The cold weather makes water pipes burst, and then there are the power outages—like the one we're having now."

"Stop!" she shouted.

He laughed. "Oh, I'm just getting started."

"Jack!" she protested, but he wasn't listening.

"It might be nice and white when it first falls, but that doesn't last long. Soon, it's stacked against the side of the road and accumulates all that dirt and grit. If that isn't bad enough, it melts and then there's flooding."

"You're raining on my parade," she said, folding her arms. He was half-teasing and she pretended to be upset.

"You mean snowing on your parade, don't you?"

"Potato, po-tat-o." Holding back a smile was nearly impossible. "Look outside." She gestured toward the window. "It's beautiful."

Jack placed his arm around her shoulders, and she leaned into him. "If you say so."

"I do."

"You're such a Pollyanna."

"That's exactly what I expect Jack Frost would say."

How long they stood staring out at the thick, white flakes floating down from the sky, Lindsay couldn't say. She felt his lips brush against her hair. Leaning back, she looked at him in the dim light of the falling snow. For a long, breath-stealing moment neither moved. Then, almost as if he couldn't stop himself, Jack leaned down and gently placed his lips on hers. His touch was light, fleeting and so tender it felt as if her heart was about to pound its way out of her chest. When he lifted his head, she wanted more. He must have read the look in her eyes, because he dropped his arms and stepped back.

Lindsay shivered, but it wasn't from the chill in the room. As if welcoming the excuse to leave her, Jack stepped away and returned with her coat, helping her into it.

"Thank you," she said, wrapping the warmth around her.

"It's late," Jack commented. "And you must be exhausted."

"I'm okay," she said, and to her embarrassment yawned.

"Come on, let's sit down." He led her back to the table. Then he went about the room and removed the white tablecloths.

"What are you doing?" she asked, curiously.

"Making you a bed."

She frowned, watching him as he spread the tablecloths on the floor, placing one on top of the other.

"Come on," he said, indicating that he wanted her to lie down.

"What about you?" she asked.

"I'll be fine."

"What time is it, anyway?" she asked and followed up with another yawn.

"It's late. Your bed awaits you, my lady." He reached for her hand and led her to the spot he'd prepared. Once she'd curled up on the makeshift mattress, he tucked her winter coat around her shoulders and then sat down beside her. "Put your head on my thigh," he said.

"I won't sleep," she insisted.

"Wanna bet?"

"No," she murmured, around yet another yawn. "I don't know why you're being so . . . nice."

"Me, neither. It goes against my nature."

"That's not true," she insisted. "You wear this bad boy image, but it's all a facade. Inside you're a cuddly teddy bear."

Jack barked a laugh. "Says the woman who believes in unicorns and fairy tales."

"I do not," she whispered. "But Bigfoot is real."

He laughed again. "Keep on thinking what you will, but trust me, I'm no teddy bear."

"If you say so." Lindsay was in no mood to argue.

Even though she'd insisted she wouldn't sleep, she did, and woke sometime later. Jack remained sitting up, his head bent uncomfortably to one side. He appeared to be sound asleep.

Taking the flashlight with her, Lindsay carefully scooted away and visited the restroom.

Jack was awake when she returned. "Did I wake you?" she asked.

"Not really."

Lindsay sank down on the floor in a sitting position next to him. They sat shoulder to shoulder. Jack wrapped his arm around her, and she leaned her head against him.

"How long do you think it'll be before we get electricity back?" she asked.

He gave a gentle shrug. "Your guess is as good as mine."

"I know this is terribly inconvenient for us both," she said with a sigh, "but I'm glad you're with me."

He kissed the top of her head. "I am, too. You might be a Pollyanna, but you're not nearly as irritating as I thought."

Coming from Jack, this was a compliment. "I feel the same about you. You're not the curmudgeon I first thought and a whole lot more likeable than I imagined."

He chuckled. "Don't get any ideas. Once we're out of here, we can each go back to the way we were."

"Really?" The thought disappointed her.

"It would be for the best, Lindsay. I told you earlier, I don't do relationships well. I have a few friends from my Marine days, but I don't see them much. I've had a girlfriend now and then, but they never lasted."

Lindsay mulled over his words and understood that while she'd gained an entirely different perspective on Jack, whatever it was they'd shared that night wasn't meant to last. It saddened her. She doubted she'd ever view him the same way, but she wouldn't go against his wishes. If that was what he wanted, then so be it.

At some point, she must have fallen asleep again, because the next thing she knew, the lights woke her. Something in the kitchen made a beeping sound.

"What was that?" she asked, sitting up and rubbing the sleep out of her eyes.

Jack was already on his feet. He went into the kitchen and Lindsay followed him. The microwave and oven were both making beeping sounds. Jack dealt with them quickly. Next, he tried the door, and it opened wide.

Turning to Lindsay, he said, "We're free. Let's get out of here."

CHAPTER 7

*L*indsay had hoped Jack would have a change of heart, but to her disappointment, she hadn't heard a peep from him in the four days since they'd left the rental hall. It felt as if he wanted to put the small intimacies they'd shared out of his mind. He might be able to do that. She, however, couldn't. Jack was in her thoughts almost constantly. It pained her to think he could so easily brush aside all that they'd shared . . . not to mention that kiss. Even now, just thinking about it gave her goosebumps. At the time, it'd felt like a promise, one that no longer seemed likely to be fulfilled.

She should have known better than to hope. Jack had made sure she understood, he didn't "do relationships." Lindsay had no option other than to abide by his wishes. She wanted to believe they'd shared something deeply personal. His silence in the days that followed told her Jack regretted mentioning anything about his father. Judging by his lack of contact since, she had to accept that he wanted matters between them to return to the way they'd once been, when they were simply polite co-workers. The only times they were likely to see each other was during their Zoom meetings.

The agency's final online meeting in December was scheduled for the morning before Christmas Eve. Lindsay had decided she wouldn't say anything about the two of them being trapped together unless he did.

Her pulse accelerated as she logged onto her home computer. It would be the first time she'd seen Jack since they'd parted outside the rental space. Jack had thoughtfully waited to be sure her car started before he'd driven away himself. Her hope soared when the small square with his photo showed at the top of her computer screen. She kept her gaze focused on him while the heads of each department gave their reports. She had no idea if he was studying her, too. When it came her turn, Brad had to say her name twice before she heard him. Embarrassed, she quickly acknowledged him and, by rote, gave her report.

Just before they logged off, Brad said, "I feel we all owe a huge debt of appreciation to Lindsay, who did such a wonderful job organizing the Christmas party. Thank you, Lindsay."

"Good job," Stephanie said.

The group went around, one by one, to offer their thanks. Lindsay paid special attention when it was Jack's turn. He looked straight at her and nodded. "You did a great job."

Lindsay waited anxiously to see if he'd say anything about what happened after the party. He didn't. Not that she'd expected he would. . .

"Have a great Christmas, everyone," Brad said, and they all signed off. Lindsay was the last one to leave the meeting, wondering, hoping, Jack would stay online, too.

He didn't.

* * *

CHRISTMAS EVE, Lindsay brought out a copy of her grandmother's gingerbread cookie recipe. It had always been one of Lindsay's favorites. She spent a good portion of the afternoon preparing the dough and rolling it out, and when she'd baked them, she decorated each one. Some of the happiest memories of her childhood were of the time she'd spent in the kitchen with her mother and grandmother, who had died that summer. Grams had lived with the family for several years, which was one reason her parents had delayed taking their anniversary cruise.

As silly as it seemed, baking those cookies gave her one small link with Jack. He'd never know she'd baked them in his honor, but that was fine. She did it for herself, too.

Lindsay was determined to make her evening as special as she could, putting up the last of the Christmas decorations she'd collected. It was hard not being with her family. On Christmas Eve, Mom always cooked a special dinner and afterward, as a family, they would attend church services. If she let herself, she could easily fall into the doldrums, and she was determined not to let that happen.

Unwilling to cook dinner, she made popcorn and sat in front of the television to watch her favorite holiday movies. Those were sure to cheer her, even if they were romances. All she wanted was for someone to have a happy ending, even if it wasn't her.

At eight, her doorbell rang. She wasn't expecting anyone but would welcome company. She opened the door to find a large dog sitting there. He gazed up at her expectantly. He had a spring of mistletoe tied to his collar.

"Hello," she greeted him. Leaning forward and looking both ways, she didn't see anyone. Getting down on one knee, she petted the dog's head. He appeared to be a golden retriever and well-groomed. "Are you lost?" she asked and searched for something that would identify the owner. Although she had to wonder how the dog had managed to ring her doorbell. . .

She located the tag on his collar that stated his name. *Oscar*. Her heart rate went into overdrive. Standing, she stepped out of her apartment trying hard to hide her excitement.

"Jack? Are you here?".

He stepped from around the corner and had a small potted poinsettia in his hand, which he thrust out at her. "I thought Oscar and I would stop by . . . if that's all right?"

It took every bit of restraint she possessed not to leap into his arms, spread kisses all over his face and hug him.

"Of course, it's all right," she said. Taking hold of Jack's arm, she pulled him inside, and Oscar followed. Lindsay set the poinsettia on the kitchen counter. Now that he was here, she wasn't about to let him leave.

Nervously, she gestured toward the sofa. "Make yourself comfortable. Can I take your coat? You aren't leaving, are you? No, you wouldn't come only to leave, right? I'm glad you brought Oscar. Are you hungry? I made popcorn for dinner, but I could throw something together, if you're interested." Thrilled as she was, she continued babbling nonsense and couldn't seem to stop.

Jack held up his hand. "We don't need anything, Lindsay."

Embarrassed, she pressed her fingertips against her mouth. She was so happy to see him that emotion clogged her throat. It'd only been five days. Five dismal days, and now that he was here, it felt overwhelming. As hard as she'd tried to put him out of her mind, she'd failed. Miserably.

"Why are you here?" she asked, when she managed to speak without a tearful display of emotion. "Don't misunderstand. I'm happy you came. More than happy. But why did you wait so long?"

Jack remained standing, with Oscar sitting obediently at his feet. As though he needed a distraction, Jack reached down to rub his ears.

He avoided eye contact. "I tried, you know."

"Tried what?"

"To stay away from you. I don't know what it is about you, Lindsay, but I can't get you out of my mind. I told you I don't do relationships."

"I know." Jack had been crystal clear about where they stood.

"I blame it on that kiss. I should've known the minute I kissed you that it was all over for me. Now I can't get you out of my head." He sounded none too pleased.

"I . . . don't know, but if it's any comfort, I haven't stopped thinking about that kiss, either . . . or about you."

He shook his head as though utterly irritated with himself and with her. "And yet I find I want to be with you more than I want to eat or sleep or anything else."

Lindsay struggled to hold back tears at the tenderness of his words.

He exhaled sharply and rubbed his hand over his face, as if to clear his thoughts. "My mother wants to meet you."

His words caught her unaware. "You told your mother about me?"

He looked away and seemed to regret mentioning it. "I did. My mother knows me better than anyone. When I showed up this evening, she knew right away that something was different with me. She wouldn't leave me alone until I told her about you. I guess you could say she's the reason I'm here."

"You didn't want to come?"

"No, I didn't. I'd rather be somewhere in outer space if you want the truth."

"Oh." That stung. For a millisecond, Lindsay was tempted to show him and his dog the door.

"My heart, however, wouldn't let me stay away another minute. Mom knew and gave me the push I needed. I want to be with you more than anything in this world, Lindsay."

Joy nearly exploded inside her. "I'm happy you went with your heart."

He shook his head as if, even now, he had doubts. "Honestly, I don't know what happened that night. I've gone over every minute we were together, trying to figure it out, and I don't have any answers. Not a one. It's like you put a spell on me. There you were, all sweetness and full of the holiday spirit, doing your utmost to make the best of the situation, while I'd done nothing but put a damper on the entire evening." His face was full of questions as if he still couldn't understand what it was about her. "I reminded myself repeatedly that the two of us aren't the least bit compatible."

Lindsay disagreed. "We seemed to be that night."

"You love Christmas and snow," he groused.

"Yes. So?"

"I hate both. You're happy, sweet, gregarious, and I'm not."

She couldn't stand being this far away from him any longer. "Jack, stop! Just stop before you talk yourself into leaving." Impulsively, she wrapped her arms around his waist and hugged him tight, savoring the moment. "I'm so happy you're here."

He glanced at the television and groaned. "Is that the Hallmark Channel?"

She nodded.

He rolled his eyes. "I should've known."

No way was she letting him leave. "Want to watch the movie with me? I've got popcorn."

He glanced at her and the television as if he couldn't believe he'd actually be willing to watch a sappy movie. He took a seat on the sofa and muttered to himself, all the while shaking his head. "I can't believe I'm doing this."

Lindsay sat down next to him, and he placed his arm around her, bringing her close. She tucked her feet to one side and leaned into him before reaching for the remote. "You won't regret it," she said, cuddling against him.

"I already do," he grumbled, and reached for the popcorn, stuffing a handful in his mouth.

"No, you don't," she insisted. He liked to pretend, but she knew he'd watch just about anything as long as she was with him.

Jack grinned. "You're right, I don't really mind. It feels good to have you in my arms. I've haven't felt like myself since I watched you drive away last week."

"You do now?" she asked, her heart longing for the truth.

"I do, but I don't like it," he muttered.

She laughed. "We both know you're lying."

He gently took hold of her chin and turned her face to his. "You don't know how badly I wanted to keep kissing you while we watched the snow fall."

"Why didn't you?" She'd longed for that very thing herself.

He shook his head as though he had his own share of regrets. "The truth? I was afraid that once I did, you'd know how deeply you affected me."

"What about now? Do you feel inclined to let loose?" She wiggled her eyebrows at him.

His frown quickly turned into a full smile. "I don't think a bulldozer could keep me away from you." Before she could draw in another breath, his mouth captured hers in the hottest kiss of her life. Lindsay twisted around so she could slip her arms around his neck. Who needed a Hallmark movie when she and Jack were in each other's arms?

And all the while, Oscar lay happily on the floor beside them.

The following morning, on Christmas Day, Jack picked her up to join his mother and sister for dinner. "Oscar's already at my mom's. I took him there first thing," he told her.

Lindsay nodded. "I'm looking forward to seeing him again." She held a platter of gingerbread cookies she wanted to bring as a hostess gift. "What's that?" Jack asked, staring down at the frosted gingerbread men.

She told him. "Would you like one?"

Lindsay knew what she was really asking, and it had nothing to do with the cookies. It was about Jack, and his willingness to let go of the pain his father had inflicted on him and his family.

He looked at the plate for a long time before he answered with another question. "Why'd you bake those?"

"They're my favorite, too." Just the way he hesitated assured her that he knew what she was asking.

He shook his head, dismissing the offer with an excuse. "I doubt they're as good as my mother's."

"You might be right, but unless you taste one, you won't find out, will you?"

After another long moment, he removed the cellophane and reached for a cookie.

Lindsay thought her heart would burst when he took the first bite.

"I always chomped off the head first," he said, with a laugh. He ate the cookie, nodded approvingly and reached for a second.

"Hey," she cried and moved the plate out of his reach. "These are for more than just you."

He laughed, kissed her soundly and led her to his vehicle. "My mother's going to love you."

"Because I'm bringing gingerbread cookies?"

"No, because she's been praying for a long time that I'd meet someone like you."

"Oh, Jack, that's the most beautiful thing you've ever said to me."

"Don't get used to it. I'm not a mushy kind of guy, spouting out words of love and drawing little hearts all over the place."

"You liked the movie last night, didn't you?" Before he could deny it, she added, "You know you did."

"Okay, fine. What I saw of it—not a lot—wasn't half bad."

"Such high praise." Although the movie hadn't been the focus of their attention. Instead, they'd been wrapped up in each other's arms and in each other's thoughts—both far more interested in kissing than watching the show.

Jack drove her to a quiet neighborhood in the north end of

Seattle. His mother's house was in the middle of the block and bright with Christmas lights glowing from the rooftop. A fully decorated tree stood in the front picture window.

Jack must have noticed her surprise. "Mom refused to let what happened with my dad ruin our Christmases. She spends a lot of time making the house as festive as she can."

"And who, pray tell, puts up those lights?"

He sighed. "Guilty as charged," he grumbled. "I don't like it, but I love my mother. She knows I'd do anything for her and so each year I dutifully put up and take down those lights."

"You're a good son."

He muttered again, as if he'd rather she didn't know he had a soft spot for his mother. But to Lindsay's way of thinking, it made him even more attractive.

Jack led her into the house. "We're here," he called out as they walked in the front door.

His mother, wearing an apron strapped around her waist, came out from the kitchen, an excited Oscar at her heels. The moment she saw Lindsay, she smiled, her entire face lighting up.

"Welcome, welcome." She held out both arms.

"Mom, this is Lindsay. Lindsay, this is my mom, Lisa."

Lindsay offered her the platter of cookies. "I'm so pleased to meet you."

His mother glanced down at the cookies and then at Jack. "It looks like someone's stolen a gingerbread man." Pointedly she stared at her son. "Was it you, Jack?"

He nodded.

For a second, it looked as though Lisa was about to weep. Her lower lip trembled as she continued to smile. "I'm glad," she finally managed to say. Then turning to Lindsay, she said, "Please make yourself at home. I'll join you in a couple of minutes. I want to get this roast in the oven."

"Can I help?" Lindsay offered.

"No, thank you, dear. I'll be out in a jiffy."

Lindsay walked over to the fireplace where a lovely garland hung. A wooden nativity set graced the mantel. Beside it were three small photos, one each of Jack and his twin sisters. Jack's must have been taken when he was a teenager, his eyes full of attitude.

"Is that really you?" she asked, turning to face him, the frame in her hand. She laughed. In the photograph, he wore a fierce, arrogant look as if defying the world.

He groaned and glanced toward the ceiling. "I had a big chip on my shoulder back then. The Marines beat that out of me in short order."

Lindsay set the photo back on the mantel and looked at the two remaining ones of his sisters. "So Beth and Emma are identical twins?"

"Yeah. I could always tell them apart, but they fooled a lot of people. Mom said when Dad returned, he tried to win them over, but they were just as eager as Mom for him to leave. He'd never been able to tell one from the other and they enjoyed frustrating him, never allowing him to know which one was which."

"I made them stop," Lisa said, coming out of the kitchen. She dried her hands on the apron.

The front door opened, and his sister burst into the room, full of laughter and life. "Hi, I'm Emma." She immediately went to Lindsay and took hold of her shoulders. "You're Lindsay?"

Lindsay nodded. "Hi," she said, laughing with delight. Instinctively she recognized that she was going to be good friends with Jack's sisters. "I'm looking forward to meeting Beth, too."

"Yeah, she called earlier today and said she can't wait to meet you."

"Maybe sometime after New Year's?"

Emma nodded, then hugged her tightly. "Thank you," she whispered.

"For?" Lindsay wasn't sure what she'd done to warrant such an enthusiastic hug.

Emma's loud laugh followed. "In appreciation for pulling my big brother's head out of his butt."

"Emma!" her mother chastised.

"Sorry, Mom." Under her breath, she added, "I'm really not." Emma wrapped her arm around Lindsay's. "I hope you know what you're in for with Jack. He can be a beast."

Lindsay looked over at Jack and watched him roll his eyes. "Stop telling fibs," he scolded his sister.

"Would I do that?" Emma asked in such an innocent way she was almost believable. "You know I love you to smithereens."

Lindsay laughed. Seeing Jack with his family meant seeing an entirely different side of him. His demeanor had completely changed. The man she'd once assumed was Jack Frost was anything but. He loved his family, and while he said he didn't "do relationships," he was willing to let down his guard and give the two of them a chance. She realized how rare what they'd shared the night of the party had been. It had gone against everything he believed about himself.

"Oh, look," Emma cried excitedly. "You're standing under mistletoe."

Both Lindsay and Jack looked up. "There's no mistletoe," Jack said.

"Pretend. I want to see you kiss Lindsay." She dropped her arm so that Lindsay stood facing Jack.

"Shall we?" Lindsay whispered.

He smiled and nodded. Bending her over his arm, he kissed her as if it was the end of World War II and they stood in the middle of Times Square. When he let her go, Lindsay's head was spinning in the most thrilling way.

Sitting down at the table for dinner, his mother asked the blessing. When Lindsay raised her head, she saw that Jack was watching her. He reached for her hand and gave it a squeeze. "I'm glad you're here," he leaned toward her and whispered.

She'd been afraid this would be the loneliest Christmas of her life. Instead, she was surrounded by Jack's family, by fun, laughter and love. Getting stuck with Jack Taylor the night of the party was turning out to be one of the best things that had ever happened to her.

SPECIAL RECIPES

* * *

From the kitchen of Debbie Macomber

Christmas Breakfast Bake
Serves 4

Need an almost hands-off holiday breakfast (or dinner)? This Christmas-inspired Hash Brown Bake has got you covered. It has crunchy hash browns, creamy eggs, and tender ham, all tossed in a sweet and tangy sauce.

Ingredients
¼ cup apricot preserves
2 teaspoons horseradish sauce
1 teaspoon Dijon mustard
¼ teaspoon garlic powder
¼ teaspoon onion powder
20-ounce package frozen shredded hash browns
3 tablespoons oil
1 teaspoon kosher salt
½ teaspoon ground black pepper
2 cups cubed ham (fully cooked)
4 eggs
2 green onions, chopped

Christmas Breakfast Bake
Continued

Directions
Preheat oven to 400°F. In a small bowl, whisk together the apricot preserves, horseradish sauce, mustard, garlic powder and onion powder. Set aside.

Toss potatoes with oil, salt and pepper on a parchment paper-lined baking sheet. Bake until edges are golden brown, 30 to 35 minutes.

Add the sauce and ham to the baking sheet, then toss to coat. With the back of a spoon, make 4 large wells in the potato mixture. Crack an egg into each well. Sprinkle eggs with salt and pepper. Bake until whites are completely set and yolks are set but not hard, 7 to 10 minutes.

Remove from oven, sprinkle green onions on top, and season with more salt and pepper to taste.

Serve immediately.

Gingerbread Bars with Cinnamon-Vanilla Frosting
Makes 16

A slightly spicy, sweet gingerbread cookie base gets topped with a melt-in-your-mouth cinnamon-vanilla frosting. These make a great gift, wrapped up and dropped on your neighbor's doorstep

Ingredients
Gingerbread Bars
2 cups flour
2 teaspoons baking soda
1 teaspoon cinnamon
1 teaspoon ground ginger
½ teaspoon kosher salt
¼ teaspoon nutmeg
¼ teaspoon allspice
½ cup (1 stick) unsalted butter, room temperature
1 ½ cups brown sugar
½ cup sugar
1/3 cup molasses
1 egg
½ teaspoon vanilla

Gingerbread Bars with Cinnamon-Vanilla Frosting
Continued

Ingredients
Cinnamon-Vanilla Frosting:
½ cup (1 stick) unsalted butter, room temperature
2 ½ cups powdered sugar
½ teaspoon cinnamon
¼ teaspoon kosher salt
3 tablespoons heavy cream or milk
½ teaspoon vanilla

Directions
Preheat oven to 350°F. Line a 9x13 inch baking pan with parchment paper and set aside.

In a medium bowl, whisk together the flour, baking soda, cinnamon, ginger, salt, nutmeg and allspice until combined. Set aside.

In the bowl of an electric mixer with the paddle attachment, beat the butter, sugars, and molasses together on medium-high speed until very light and fluffy, 2 - 3 minutes. Add the egg and vanilla; mix to combine. Slowly add the dry ingredients, and mix just until combined. Dough will be sticky.

Gingerbread Bars with Cinnamon-Vanilla Frosting
Continued

Directions
Scrape dough into the parchment-lined baking pan. Place a piece of plastic wrap on top of the dough, then use your hands to spread evenly on the bottom of the pan. Remove plastic wrap and discard.

Bake for 25 - 30 minutes, until puffed and almost set (it will jiggle slightly in the middle). Place on a cooling rack to cool completely.

Meanwhile, make the frosting. In the bowl of an electric mixer with the paddle attachment, beat the butter on medium speed until creamy, about 1 minute. Add half of the powdered sugar, and all of the cinnamon and salt; beat on low until absorbed. Add the heavy cream and vanilla; beat on low until creamy. Add the rest of the powdered sugar on low until absorbed. Once combined, beat on medium speed until fluffy and slightly lighter in color, about 1 minute. Spread on cooled gingerbread bars. Sprinkle with additional cinnamon.

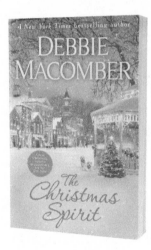
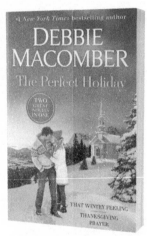

ABOUT THE AUTHOR

DEBBIE MACOMBER is a leading voice in women's fiction, with more than 200 million copies of her books in print worldwide. Twelve of her novels have hit #1 on the *New York Times* bestseller list, with three debuting at #1 on the *New York Times*, *USA Today*, and *Publishers Weekly* lists.

debbiemacomber.com